First Grade Valentines

by Joanne Ryder

Pictures by Betsy Lewin

Troll Associates

Library of Congress Cataloging-in-Publication Data

Ryder, Joanne.
    First grade valentines / by Joanne Ryder; illustrated by Betsy
Lewin.
        p.   cm. (First grade is the best!)
    Summary: The children in Mrs. Lee's first grade class make cards,
cookies, and paper animals for Valentine's Day. Includes step-by-
step instructions for making an origami bunny.
    ISBN 0-8167-3004-0 (lib. bdg.)   ISBN 0-8167-3005-9 (pbk.)
    [1. Valentine's Day—Fiction. 2. Schools—Fiction.] I. Lewin,
Betsy, ill. II. Title. III. Series.
PZ7.R423Fi 1993
[E]—dc20   92-35388

With loving thanks to the children and teachers of Centre Avenue School in East
Rockaway, New York and Marshall School and Bryant School of Dubuque, Iowa for
all their valentine thoughts and friendly ideas.

JR

One morning there was a big box
in the first grade room.

"I wonder what's inside," Meg
whispered.

"I can read the sign on it," said
Lisa. "I LOVE YOU."

Their teacher, Mrs. Lee, smiled at the children.

"This is a holiday box," Mrs. Lee told the class. "Who knows what holiday comes next week?"

"Valentine's Day!" said Gabe.

"Yes," said Mrs. Lee. "It's a special day for friends and a time for sharing with others. The things in this holiday box will help us get ready for Valentine's Day."

Mrs. Lee opened the big box.
Inside were sheets of red and pink
paper and lots of envelopes.
  "This looks like fun," said Robin.
The first graders cut out hearts.

They put hearts everywhere.
"Here's one for you, Martha,"
said Katie.

She taped a red heart above the
bunny's cage.

The next day, Mrs. Lee gave each
child a box of candy hearts.

"You can eat them later," she
said. "Let's count them now."

The children put the colored hearts
in piles. They counted each pile.

Then they filled in boxes on a chart to show how many they counted. The pink had the most boxes.

"I'm glad," said Matt. "The pink ones taste the best."

Later that day, the children printed their names on white paper bags. Now everyone knew where to deliver their valentines.

Katie drew a picture of Martha on her valentine bag.

Lisa drew four playful cats on hers.

"Those are nice cats," Katie said. "You must love cats as much as I love bunnies."

"Yes," said Lisa. "I wish I had a cat. I'd call him Tiger."

"My cat is fat," said Meg. "She's going to have kittens."

"I LOVE kittens," said Lisa.

"Mama says Posy will have kittens
any day," Meg said.

Lisa helped Meg draw a fat, smiling
cat with kittens on her valentine bag.

The children shared all the things in the big box. They made cards for their families.

Mrs. Lee made some, too.

"This one is for my neighbor,"
she said. "She fell and broke her hip.
Now I feed her birds every day."

"Is she sad?" asked Robin.
"When I had the flu, I was sad."

"Yes," said Mrs. Lee. "She is sad
and a little lonely."

"I can make her a card with
birds," said Nick.

Soon each child made a cheery card.

"Thank you," said Mrs. Lee.

"These will make her feel better."

The first graders made cards at home, too. They each brought home a list of all their classmates. Brian's mother showed him how to fold paper animals for his valentines.

"This bunny is for Katie," he said. "She likes bunnies, and I like her."

Matt and his twin, Mike, made
their valentines together. Their cards
looked alike.

"No one will know," said Matt,
"since we are in different first grade
classes."

Just before Valentine's Day, the children made cookies. They covered the hearts with pink icing.

"Oh, yummy," said Gabe, licking his fingers. "I can't wait until the party tomorrow."

On Valentine's Day, the first
graders had a great time.

They put cards in each other's
valentine bags.

Everyone got lots of valentines.
Even Martha!

They read their cards, and they ate their cookies.

"The penguin you gave me is neat," Nick told Brian.

"I can show you how to make it," Brian said.

"I'll make one for my dad," said Nick. "He loves penguins."

"I liked your card," Robin told Matt. "Your brother sent me the same kind."

"Oh," said Matt, and he smiled.

"Look at all our cards," said Meg.

"Look at all my funny bunnies," said Katie.

There was a bunny on each of her valentines!

The next day, the children had a
special time for sharing.

"My neighbor loved your cards,"
Mrs. Lee said. "When she can, she
wants to visit and meet her first
grade valentines."

"Your neighbor will be our new friend," said Robin.

"That's right," said Mrs. Lee. "On Valentine's Day, it's nice to remember our old friends. But it's nice to make new ones, too."

"I have news," called Meg. "Posy
had four kittens."

"How sweet!" said Mrs. Lee.
"You have new friends, too."

Meg gave Lisa a big envelope.
Inside was a photo of a kitten and a
heart. On the heart, it said, TIGER
LOVES LISA!

"He's yours," said Meg. "When
he's bigger, you can take him home.
My mama called your mama, and
it's okay."

"Hooray!" cried Lisa. She hugged
the photo and her friend.

"What a purr-fect valentine," said Gabe.

The first graders laughed. But they knew Gabe was right. Tiger was the best valentine of all.

Make an origami bunny with floppy ears—just like Martha!

You will need a square piece of paper, child-safe scissors, and crayons or markers.

1. Fold your paper like this. Then open.

2. Fold along dotted lines toward crease in middle.

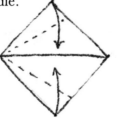

3. Fold along dotted line.

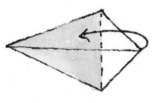

4. Cut along line AB. These will be your bunny ears.

5. Fold back on dotted line. This will be your bunny tail.

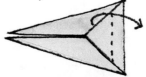

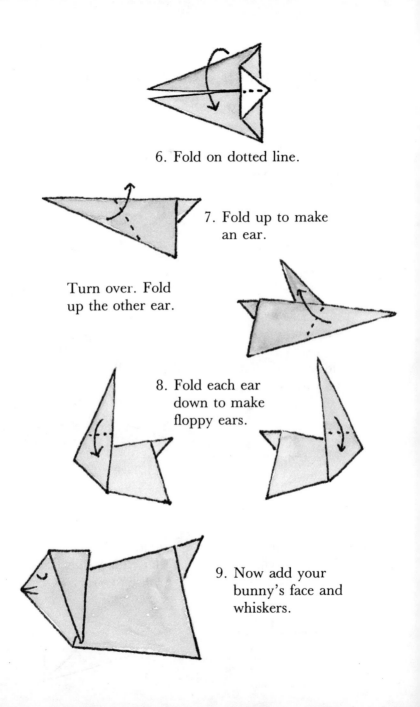

6. Fold on dotted line.

7. Fold up to make an ear.

Turn over. Fold up the other ear.

8. Fold each ear down to make floppy ears.

9. Now add your bunny's face and whiskers.